Thieves from Space

Thieves from Space

BY E.T. RANDALL

Illustrations by Jackie Rogers

TROLL ASSOCIATES

Library of Congress Cataloging in Publication Data

Randall, E.T.
    Thieves from space.

    (Alien adventures)
    Summary: The reader may choose the direction of the
plot as aliens from outer space arrive on Earth,
purportedly to warn of a terrible disaster.
        1. Plot-your-own stories.   2. Children's stories,
American.   [1. Science fiction.   2. Extraterrestrial
beings—Fiction.   3. Plot-your-own stories]   I. Rogers,
Jacqueline, ill.   II. Title.   III. Series.
PZ7.R1564Th   1985   [Fic]   84-8538
ISBN 0-8167-0330-2 (lib. bdg.)
ISBN 0-8167-0331-0 (pbk.)

10   9   8   7   6   5   4   3   2   1

Before You Begin
Your Alien Adventure...

Remember—this is an out-of-this-world book. Start on page 1 and keep reading till you come to a choice. After that, the story is up to you. As you make decisions, your adventure will take you from page to page.

Think carefully before you decide! Some choices will lead you to exciting, heroic, and happy endings. But watch out! Other choices can quickly lead to disaster.

Now you're ready to begin. Best of luck in your **Alien Adventure!**

Thieves from Space

You are delivering newspapers in the early morning hours of a quiet Saturday. The weather is crisp and clear. You are full of energy. Eager to finish your paper route early, you race down the block on your bike.

As you toss your first paper, you notice the mailbox on the house has been turned upside down. It looks strange, hanging there with the top open.

Halfway down the block, you see a metal fence twisted into the shape of a figure eight. "Wow, what a weird sculpture," you say to yourself.

Next comes the house where the St. Bernard dog always chases you. He thinks it's a great game when you fall off your bike and rip your jeans. "Some game," you think. "He has all the fun." Well, he's not going to make you fall today. You're ready for him.

There's his bark. But where is he? Wait a minute; why is he sitting on the roof of the house? And what's that funny whirring sound?

You turn around and see an emerald-green ray zipping back and forth across the street. Everything it touches, vanishes. Faster and faster it moves.

It's coming straight at you!

Turn to page 2.

2

The beam moves so rapidly that your eyes can't follow it. Suddenly the ray strikes the car next to you. The car vanishes! Instead of moving on, the beam stops. It is vibrating as though it is alive.

The beam expands and contracts, turning different shades of green. First it is the bright green of a lime. Then it is the dull green of an olive. You never realized how many colors green could be. Soon the color changes are too rapid for your eyes to follow. But throughout the display, the beam has not moved.

It seems to be studying you. Then you notice that the pulsing of the beam mirrors your breathing. As you inhale, the beam expands. As you exhale, the beam contracts. You sense its power and strength, and wonder if it's dangerous.

If you are curious and want to investigate, turn to page 7.

If you go to get help, turn to page 19.

If you wish to cautiously test the beam's power, turn to page 26.

Chances are that it's Mom, so you go back to answer the phone. As you pick it up, a sharp metallic voice says, "The master is dying. Hurry!"

"Who is this?" you ask.

"I am the voice of Meglar's computer. Hurry. The master needs your help."

You hang up the phone and race outside. When you get to Meglar, he is barely breathing. His red skin confuses you. Where should you spread the lotion? As you look at him, you notice that certain patches of his skin are darker than others. You apply the lotion and hope you're not too late.

Meglar's eyes open and his lips crinkle in a smile. "Thank you, Earthling, you have saved my life with this primitive salve. I am in your debt."

You help Meglar into his spaceship. "I have long been curious about Earthlings, and I wanted to meet one," he says. "As I was taking samples of your civilization to study, my sensors detected a human presence. So I brought you here. If all Earthlings have your courage, I have discovered a planet of heroes. I must leave now and report my findings to my home planet. I will return."

When you are safely away from the ship, it takes off and is gone. Now, every time you see a blinking light in the sky, you wonder if it is your friend Meglar returning to Earth.

THE END

Since the alien is unconscious, you run to the spaceship hoping to find more aliens to help you. As you enter the ship, a metallic voice challenges you.

"Stop. Do not come any closer."

"Who are you?" you ask.

"I am computer GX4 of the Starsearch Class..."

"I need help," you interrupt. "Meglar has fallen into a poisonous plant. He's dying."

"Describe the plant."

You do the best you can. Then the computer directs you to the ship's lab. There, an android prepares an antidote.

With the finished antidote in your hand, you rush outside. You hold Meglar's head and let him drink the liquid. At first, nothing happens. Then his body quivers and goes stiff.

Did the computer give you the wrong formula? Should you stay with Meglar, or should you try to verify the formula with the ship's computer?

If you run back to the ship to check with the computer, turn to page 62.

If you stay with Meglar, turn to page 9.

Deciding to investigate, you carefully pedal your bike closer to the beam. You wonder what will happen if you touch it. Slowly you reach out. Instantly, the beam zaps you in its green glow. Your bike is transformed into a clear plastic bubble. Then the bubble surrounds you!

The bubble whizzes you away at high speed. "Terrific," you think. "I had to touch it. Now what's going to happen to me?"

"Oh no!" You are going to crash into the trees in the woods behind town. Before you can duck, the bubble skirts in and out of the trees, throwing you off balance.

Just as you sit back and begin to enjoy the ride, the bubble crashes through a clump of thick brush and stops abruptly.

You can't believe your eyes. In front of you stands a huge spacecraft. Gleaming silver in the sunlight, the ship is shaped like a lamp shade—wide and circular on the bottom, tapering to a small circle on top. There are no windows or doors of any kind facing you. The craft begins to glow, and the brightness hurts your eyes.

Slowly a rectangle traces itself onto the hull of the ship. It is a hatch, and it begins to open.

Turn to page 29.

from page 82

As you and Meglar wait, the mayor comes to the jail. He believes your story and contacts Washington. You speak on the phone with the President of the United States. "Our scientists have known about the deadly comet," says the President. "The problem was, we were powerless to stop it."

With Meglar's help, the people of Earth are quickly evacuated to their new planet.

One day, Meglar visits you with three other Space Guardians.

They all bow solemnly to you and Meglar speaks. "Earthling, you risked much to save your planet. In doing so, you have earned the right to be a Space Guardian. Will you join us?"

"Will I?" you say. A whole universe of adventure opens before you. "Of course I will!"

THE END

from page 5

You decide to stay with Meglar. The alien's skin color slowly returns to normal. His eyes snap open, and he studies you before speaking.

"Thank you, Earthling," he says. "You have saved my life."

The alien tries to stand, but he is too wobbly. You help him back into his spaceship. Gently, you lead him to a chair on the bridge of his ship. He looks tired and stares at you through sad eyes.

"Will you be okay?" you ask.

"I will be fine. It is the Earth that is in danger. My foolish accident has wasted precious time. I am a Space Guardian, sent to your planet to warn you of a terrible disaster.

"Guardians like myself have been protecting the universe for generations. All of us are survivors of planets that were destroyed. Our duty is to warn other planets in danger. And, believe me, your Earth is threatened."

Turn to page 74.

10

from page 98

As you run through the gate, you hear the dog growling once again. A loud crash rings out, sounding like garbage cans being knocked over. Another strange sound rings out behind you. "Whoop, whoop, whoop," the high-pitched cry repeats. It must be the alien's voice.

This is your chance to escape. Yet you have a feeling the alien is in danger. "Even though he looks weird," you think, "he really hasn't hurt me." Again the alien cries out. "I've got to find out what's happening to him."

You return to the yard and see the alien sitting on a tree branch wailing like a baby. Beneath him, the dog is prowling around the base of the tree, pushing the ball with his nose, then leaping high into the air at the frightened alien.

The alien sees you and cries out. "Help me. Please help me."

Behind you is escape, but the alien's cries of distress make you feel sorry for him. What should you do?

If you escape, turn to page 57.

If you help the alien, turn to page 69.

You freeze in your tracks. Meglar presses his belt buckle, transporting you to his side. "You are safe now," he says. "Watch." He tosses an old test tube at the computer. A yellow light vaporizes the object. Amazing!

"The computer is programmed to neutralize anything that gets too close to its protective field. I'm glad you stopped. You saw what it did to that test tube. But what made you run in the first place?" Meglar looks puzzled.

"You're a robot," you say. "You've got wires inside."

"I am not a robot," says Meglar. "I'm an android. There's a difference, you know. Robots are cold, mechanical creatures who are incapable of independent thought. We androids are capable of reasoning, just like our creators. We are rightfully proud of our independence. But you have not answered my question. Why did you run?"

"I never saw a rob... er, android before, and I didn't know what you were going to do to me."

Meglar laughs. "You helped me to repair my circuits. I was going to keep my part of our bargain."

"There really is a formula?"

"Of course there is. Androids can't lie. It runs counter to our programming. I will write out the formula for you. It is really very simple. I wonder why you humans didn't think of it before."

Turn to page 107.

"I don't believe your story," you say. "I'm not going to help you."

Meglar's smile vanishes. In seconds, you are encased in the red vapor. The more you struggle to get free, the tighter you are held.

Meglar studies you through the mist as though you were a specimen in a laboratory. He pushes at the mist, and it rolls like a beach ball. Over and over you go until you get quite dizzy.

Meglar rolls you onto his ship and puts you into a glass-lined box. A cold chill creeps into your box, freezing your feet, your legs, and finally your whole body.

"You were foolish not to help me. At least you would have remained free. Know this, Earthling, while you still can hear me. Your planet is rich in gold, silver, and diamonds. My mining beam will soon be perfected and I will find Earth's treasures. But for now, you are the greater prize. You will fetch me a handsome price from the miners on Pera-Linc. They are always looking for strong young workers."

Meglar is freezing you in suspended animation for the long space voyage. The last sound you hear is the alien's shrill laughter.

THE END

14

You decide you must resist. The alien steps aside to let you walk in front of him. As you pass by, you shove him to the ground.

You are in a well-lit underground cavern. You run towards a large, slightly open steel door.

It looks like you're going to make it. But suddenly a gigantic hand slams the door shut. You try to escape from the hand, but it closes around you and lifts you high into the air. You look around, expecting to see a giant. There is only the hand.

The hand drops you at Wulnar's feet. "You almost escaped, Earthling. I will not underestimate you again."

Turn to page 92.

16

from page 38

You toss the piece of wood. It clatters on the floor and raises a swirling cloud of dust. The alien races forward. The rotten floorboards crack under him. He crashes through the floor! But the alien himself doesn't make a sound. You wait a couple of minutes. What's going on down there? Curious, you edge towards the hole.

Wait a minute. You don't really want to see what happened to the alien. All you want to do is get out of this creepy house. But your curiosity gets the better of you.

You peer into the hole and find yourself looking straight into the glowing eyes of the floating alien. Mini-rockets attached to his belt kept him from falling. Now his tentacle wraps around you, pulling you close to him.

"You're a bit scrawny," he says, "but you'll do." The last thing that you see is the razor-sharp teeth of the alien as he opens his hungry mouth.

THE END

You don't believe Meglar's story. You refuse to help him. Muttering to himself, the alien clutches your arm and straps you into a seat.

He activates the controls and the ship shoots far out into space. The G-forces press you deeper into your seat. You wonder what Meglar is going to do.

"Put on this space suit," commands the alien. "We are going for a walk." Outside of the ship, you float in space. It feels like being underwater.

You turn your head and see hundreds of spacecraft approaching Earth. Beyond them is a fiery streak that lights up the darkness of space. The alien was telling the truth.

"Now will you help?" asks Meglar.

"I'll help," you say, hoping that you can save Earth from the certain disaster it faces.

THE END

You decide to get help. As you turn your bike around, the beam lashes out at you. You stumble and drop your bike. The beam engulfs and vaporizes your bike.

You run up the block as fast as you can. Suddenly, you crash into something and fall to the ground. It's an invisible barrier!

You try to feel your way around the barrier, but it seems to stretch all the way across the street. As you pause to think, a short, fat, orange creature materializes before you.

His face is wrinkled like a prune and his head is bald. He has three eyes in the center of his face. There's no sign of any ears or a nose or a mouth. As you stare at him, a tentacle wraps itself around your arm.

Desperately you pull free and run into someone's driveway. Maybe you can find shelter in the backyard. To your right is a snarling Doberman pinscher guarding an open gate. To your left is a high wooden fence. In front of you is a garage with an open door. Behind you is the alien. Which way do you go?

If you want to get by the dog, turn to page 98.

If you want to hop the fence, turn to page 52.

If you want to go into the garage, turn to page 37.

from page 45

As the fire burns out of control, you try to escape. Flaming androids are running everywhere. You search for the android carrying Orv, but you can't find him. Ahead of you is a steel door that is starting to close.

You race for the door and fling yourself towards the shrinking opening. You made it!

You're now in a long corridor. Is that daylight at the end of it? You run as fast as you can, and in minutes you are in the open. The sunlight striking your face never felt so reassuring.

But where are you? You look around and see that you are in the abandoned quarry outside of town. As you run to get help, a terrific explosion rocks the ground.

The shock wave knocks you off your feet. When you stand up, you see a huge crater where the quarry used to be. You hear sirens and see fire trucks speeding toward you.

The debris from the Earthbase falls from the sky like raindrops. You dodge back and forth to avoid getting hit. You wonder how you will explain how all those android arms and legs got here.

As you search the wreckage, hoping that Orv survived, you see an object glittering in the sunlight. It is a diamond. You're rich!

THE END

What the heck, you figure. You point your finger and aim at the alien. "Zap," you say. To your utter surprise, a lavender ray streaks from your finger and misses the alien by inches.

The surprised alien dives away from you. You stare in disbelief at your finger. As the alien lifts his head, you zap him again and another ray shoots over him.

The alien scientist scrambles for cover, and you chase him around the underground base. He has his hands over his head and his tentacle flaps behind him as he ducks from the blasts from your finger. You don't know how a loaded finger is possible, but you continue to pursue the alien, hoping to find a way out of this underground maze.

You remember how frightened you were when the alien was after you. Now you are a bit ashamed that you are doing the same thing to the alien.

Without any warning, the brown mist returns and snakes its way up your body. But something else is happening. A cry rings out from the alien. The mist is enclosing him, too.

Turn to page 114.

You materialize in what seems to be a laboratory. Meglar hurries to a streamlined, crystaline work bench. As he works, you take a look around.

The room is pure white. On the wall behind you is a huge computer. You can see messages flashing on its viewing screen in a strange language. The work bench is filled with an unusual assortment of instruments. One of them looks like a pocket comb, yet Meglar is using it as a torch to cut through the lead. You hope that Meglar will let you explore his ship. There is much that you want to see.

Finally Meglar is finished. Turning to you, he holds a bunch of hair-thin lead wires. He calmly unzips his jump suit, exposing his blinking circuitry. Meglar is a robot!

You let out a gasp and back away. Suddenly you are afraid of the alien. Meglar calls out to you.

"Stop. Don't go any further."

If you stop, turn to page 12.

If you ignore him, turn to page 33.

As you press the black button, you and the robot are transported to the bridge of the spaceship. Rebex is laughing. Qwoc is manning the controls of the ship.

"What have we here?" asks Rebex, clearly surprised to see you. The robot explains how you saved him. Rebex listens carefully. "Well, maybe you can be useful to us."

"What do you want with me?" you ask.

"Qwoc and I can use a humanoid assistant to scout a planet before we rob it. One who has courage, with just the right amount of curiosity."

"But I'm no thief," you say.

"No problem. We will modify your behavior."

You try to change the subject. "What are you doing to Earth?" you ask. "You're stealing everything."

"Not everything. Qwoc eats metal. He has a tremendous appetite. We have taken what we need." Rebex points to a viewing screen. "Now, gaze on your home, Earthling, for the last time."

As you stare at the screen, a soft voice echoes in your brain. Your thoughts are rearranged. You are now an eager assistant of Rebex and Qwoc.

THE END

from page 99

The antenna on Rebex's head waves back and forth. Have you angered him?

"Earthling, we are not thieves," says Rebex. "We simply borrowed a few things that we will return when the hunt is over."

"But you can't just take things that don't belong to you," you point out.

"Earthling, it is unfortunate that the effects of Qwoc's eyes are temporary. In your case, it would be a blessing if you forgot how to talk. Are you ready to go home?"

Before you can answer, an explosion rocks the spaceship. The lights flicker, and both aliens race for the instrument panels. Warning lights are blinking and alarms are sounding. As the aliens struggle to save their ship, a flickering series of yellow lights appears behind them.

As you watch in fascination, the lights take the shape of a small being. You want to warn Rebex and Qwoc, but you are annoyed that they played a trick on you.

Another explosion jars the ship as the yellow light becomes more solid. What do you do?

If you warn the aliens, turn to page 46.

If you remain silent, turn to page 28.

26

You decide to test the power of the beam by throwing a rock at it. The rock disappears! You move back a step.

When you throw one of your newspapers at the beam, the paper goes right through it, landing in the street beyond the beam. Now how did that happen?

"Wait a minute," you think. Most of the strange things you saw on your paper route were made of metal—except for the dog on the roof. You have an idea for an experiment.

You reach into your pocket and find a penny and a piece of gum. You throw them both toward the beam simultaneously. The gum lands in the street and the penny vanishes. "Hmmm," you think. "The beam takes some things and not others. Why?"

You drop your bike and approach the beam, careful not to get too close. You want to study it. It still hasn't moved, but touching it might be dangerous. As you stand gazing at the beam, you feel a gentle tugging at your belt buckle, pulling you closer to the strange light.

Just as you realize what is happening, the beam snatches you from the sidewalk.

Turn to page 71.

from page 68

Pretending to go wild, you fall down and spin like a top. You bray like a donkey and kick up your back legs.

Your behavior startles the alien. He looks confused. You are determined to keep him off balance. You get to your knees and pretend to be a dog. You bark and leap high into the air.

The alien doesn't look so confident now. He casts a nervous glance around the chamber, as though looking for a place to hide. You straighten up and walk stiffly toward the alien.

"I am the Frankenstein monster," you cry. You hold your arms in front of you and shuffle straight at the alien.

He lets out a yelp of panic and tries to hide behind an instrument panel. You laugh as the alien cowers. Suddenly, his attitude changes.

"Do not laugh at me, Earthling. I will not be made a fool of," he screams. He presses a button on the instrument console. Red beams zip over your head. You duck and they barely miss you. Now what?

On the floor are several glass discs. You pick one up and throw it at the alien. The disc shatters against the instrument panel and makes half of it invisible! You grab two more discs and run for cover as the alien comes after you.

Turn to page 61.

from page 25

You remain silent as the lights transform into a blond boy with an evil-looking scar running down his cheek. He holds up a platinum triangle. The strange device emits a blue net which wraps you securely in its grasp. An instant later, both Rebex and Qwoc are also immobilized.

More blinking lights form into humanoids, and they all gather around the blond boy. He seems to be their leader. The boy listens for a few moments, then silences the humanoids with a wave of his hand. He is only four feet tall, but he seems to hold great power.

He releases you from the webbing. "I am Syncron Zim. And these are my men. What are you doing with these two petty thieves? Are they your traveling companions?"

When you explain, Syncron frowns. "Hmm," he says, rubbing his cheek. "The cargo of this vessel is worthless, not even worth hijacking. But there are riches on Earth that we can take before destroying the planet." He smiles wickedly.

In desperation, you lunge for Syncron, but he is too fast for you. The blue webbing encases you again. Now Syncron is angry.

Turn to page 49.

from page 7

A ramp drops from the spacecraft and a tall, red alien with green hair appears.

He walks down the ramp, pressing his belt buckle. The plastic bubble around you vanishes. You drop to the ground. On first impulse, you're ready to run. But when you see the alien smiling, you become confused. Perhaps the smile is genuine. Yet you feel a vague mistrust of this peculiar-looking stranger.

He gets closer to you, and you see that his eyes are practically all white. His stare seems to bore holes right through you. You are uncomfortable, yet you can't draw your eyes away from the alien's gaze. It's as though he is hypnotizing you.

If you could get to that clump of brush, you might be able to escape. But your curiosity about this being makes you want to question him. The alien stops, as though waiting for you to decide what to do. The chirping of a bird draws his eyes away from you. Now's your chance.

If you run to the brush, turn to page 34.

If you greet the alien, turn to page 47.

You sit in a comfortable chair, contoured to fit your body. Meglar's sure hands pilot the spaceship. You see the Earth on a large viewing screen in front of you.

"This phase of my mission," says Meglar, "is to chart topography and population density.

"There are many more people here than before," says Meglar as he views a sports stadium on his scanner. "Look at that. People are fighting just to have some open space."

"They aren't fighting. They're playing football," you reply.

"What's football?"

You explain the game to Meglar, and he shakes his head in amazement.

He lands the ship under water and takes you with him to map the ocean floor. You see strange ruins of a long-forgotten civilization. "This used to be Atlantis," Meglar says. "I see it sank."

Later, as you streak over the Grand Canyon, Meglar announces that his survey is completed. He transports you back to your neighborhood.

You run home, bursting to tell your adventures to your mother. "What have you been up to?" she asks. "You've been gone for two hours. And how did you get those marks on your forehead?"

With a sigh, you realize that Mom—and everyone else—will never believe your story.

THE END

from page 116

As you sit in the dark, you look back and see a figure slip quietly into the room. You hold your breath, not daring to give away your hiding spot. Not five feet away, you hear a scrape on the floor.

You don't move, and the sound passes on. Suddenly, the room is bathed in brightness! An alien is standing in front of you holding a glowing cube in his hand. You blast him with the paralyzer. Now only Zim is left.

The next room is behind a black curtain. It leads to a slide, exiting the Fun House. Even though Zim could be waiting below, you decide to chance the slide. It is your only way out.

"Ready or not, here I come," you think. You slide down and land in a sawdust pit. You quickly duck out of sight. Suddenly Zim walks right by, looking up at the slide. He just missed seeing you. You pull out your paralyzer and fire, missing Zim by inches. He turns around. Before he can return your fire, you zap him.

The hour is up. You've won!

THE END

from page 22

You ignore Meglar's warning. All you want to do is get away from him. You keep backing up, keeping your eyes glued to him.

"Don't move," Meglar commands. "You are getting too close to the ship's computer system. It has a self-defense mechanism that will destroy any intruder who gets too close—"

Too late. You are vaporized in a puff of blue smoke.

THE END

34

You dash toward the trees for safety, hearing the alien's high-pitched laughter behind you. Ice-blue bolts whoosh over your head. As they pass, you can hear the air crackle with electricity. You throw yourself to the ground, just in time. The blue rays miss you by a hair.

"I've got to find something to defend myself," you think. The alien is coming toward you. He is speaking into a circular device in his palm. You can understand every word he says.

"Forgive me, Earthling. I only meant to amuse you with my powers. Stand up. I won't hurt you."

"Some joke," you think. "But I'm not laughing." You remain on the ground trying to hide behind a fallen tree. If only you could defend yourself. As you look around, you see a broken branch behind you. It looks like a club. To your left is a large flat stone.

If you pick up the branch, turn to page 72.

If you pick up the stone, turn to page 110.

from page 58

You decide to touch the beam, hoping it will transport you back to Earth.

The beam flashes and deposits a load of garbage cans which barely miss you. At the same instant, it plucks you from your feet and bathes you in a sea of green.

"It worked," you think. "I'm going home."

It is your last thought. The beam is locked on a "collect" setting. It won't transport anything back to Earth. Instead of going home, you are turned into a frying pan. The beam deposits you onto an ever-growing pile of cooking utensils.

THE END

36

from page 102

You follow the robot to the steel door. As the door opens, you meet Rebex standing on the other side. He is quite surprised to see you. Before he can reach for his weapon, the robot immobilizes him by encasing him in a block of ice.

"How did you do that?" you ask.

"I have liquid-oxygen cartridges that I use as a self-defense mechanism. It is stored at such a low temperature that when released it turns to ice."

"What about Qwoc?" you ask.

"He will not dare to leave the controls on the bridge. We will have plenty of time to make our escape."

The robot leads you down a long corridor, and you find yourself on the ship's hangar deck. As the robot readies a small craft for takeoff, you wonder if your escape attempt will succeed.

"Secure your seat harness, master." A roar fills the hangar deck as an outer door opens. Ahead of you is the vastness of space. You never realized that there were so many stars. The ship lurches forward.

It feels like a roller-coaster ride as the robot maneuvers the small spacecraft through a series of loops and dives. When he levels off, you see the Earth ahead of you.

You're home! And you have a new friend . . .

THE END

from page 19

You run into the garage and hide behind an old automobile. You hope that the darkness of the garage will hide you from the alien. As you cautiously peek out, the door slowly opens.

The alien is framed in the bright daylight. You can't make out his features exactly, but you see that he is holding some kind of weapon in his hand. You hold your breath as the alien steps into the garage.

"Come out, Earthling. There is no escape."

You gasp. He knows you are here.

Or is he only bluffing, hoping that you will reveal your hiding place?

If you try to run for it, turn to page 88.

If you remain hidden, turn to page 60.

from page 52

Racing up the stairs to the second floor, you nearly trip over a pile of canvas and rope bundled in the shadows at the top of the landing. Your foot crashes through the rotted flooring. That gives you an idea. If you can lure the alien up here, maybe you can take him prisoner.

Stomping your feet on the floor, you try to make enough noise to attract the alien. But you have to be careful not to go through the floor again. The canvas and rope can be useful, so you drag them into a dark corner. Then you wait for the alien.

You hear footsteps on the stairs. So far, so good.

The alien reaches the landing. As he searches for you in the gloom, his eyes glow like fog lights. Back and forth the amber eyes track, as systematically as an aircraft beacon. Now they focus in your direction. Your heart is hammering in your chest.

"Maybe this isn't such a good idea after all," you think. As the alien gets closer, you shrink deeper into the shadows. Your hand brushes against a piece of wood. Should you toss it at him? Or should you remain silent?

If you toss the wood, turn to page 16.

If you remain silent, turn to page 89.

You decide to go for help. First you must drag Meglar out of the poison ivy. Even though he is tall, he is surprisingly light. But not light enough to carry all the way home. You race off to get help on your own.

As you run, you try to remember what the nurse used when you caught poison ivy in camp. The medicine was pink, and you had to wear it all the time. You hop the fence to your backyard and go through the back door.

Calamine lotion! That was the name of the medicine. You dash to the bathroom, grab the bottle from the medicine cabinet and run to the door.

Just as you are about to leave the house, the telephone rings. "It could be Mom," you think. She'd be able to help. But time is running out. Meglar could be dying. The phone rings again.

If you answer the phone, turn to page 4.

If you don't stop, turn to page 79.

You tell Meglar your name, and he repeats it twice, as though familiarizing himself with its sound. His face grows serious.

"I need your help," he says.

"I won't help you as long as I'm a prisoner," you reply.

Your response amuses Meglar, and he laughs heartily. He points a device shaped like a tuning fork at you, and the red mist melts away. You can once again move your hands and feet.

"Now that you are free, you must tell how I can obtain five ounces of lead."

"Why do you need lead?" you ask.

"During a magnetic storm in space, the lead wiring in my ship's navigational system burned out. It must be replaced if I am ever to return to my own planet. It is not my intention to steal that which is not mine, but I have no other way to fix my craft without frightening the people of your planet. If you assist me, I promise that I will give you a formula which can change water into fuel."

If you agree to help, turn to page 50.

If you refuse to help, turn to page 13.

"If you let me go, I promise I won't tell anyone what you are doing," you say.

"Promises can be broken, Earthling."

"Why don't you keep me a prisoner until you are finished?" you suggest. "Then when you leave, I can go free."

"You can always escape."

"Why don't you erase my memory and then leave me back on my block? If I don't remember what happened, how can I say anything?"

Shaking like jelly, Wulnar laughs in deep grunts. "Earthling, I have no power to erase your memory. Enough! You are tiring me with these impractical plans. There is only one solution." The alien reaches into his belt and pulls out a large teardrop-shaped diamond.

The diamond begins glowing and you shield your eyes from the brightness. A strange tingling sensation flows through your body.

Opening your eyes, you discover that you have shrunk to microscopic size and are trapped forever inside the diamond.

THE END

As you walk with Meglar, you realize that you are still holding the emerald crystal. "Why didn't he take it back?" you wonder. Your path is blocked by thick underbrush, but Meglar never hesitates. One long step takes him over the brush.

The emerald crystal glows in your hand. Suddenly you are lifted gently over the brush, too. "He controls me through the crystal," you say to yourself.

Your feet touch the ground. "This is my chance," you think. You throw the crystal away and start to run. Which way should you go? The brush gives you good cover. But you could move faster on the trail.

If you crash through the brush, turn to page 106.

If you take the trail, turn to page 56.

"Earthling, you have nothing to fear. You will be released when my mission is completed."

"Why can't I go now?" you ask.

"Every time my race has tried to make contact with your planet, we have been attacked. So, we decided to avoid contact with your kind until you were ready to meet us. I must leave you now. I have wasted far too much time talking to you. Every second is precious, and I must return to my work. You may investigate my base, but you cannot leave yet. Two androids will be your guardians."

You explore the secret Earthbase. The vast base is piled high with metal objects of every description. Some are mixing chemicals. Others bring more metal to be melted down in a huge roaring furnace.

The heat from the furnace is stifling. You feel as though the air itself is on fire. You move back quickly and notice that one of the androids has started to smoke. Suddenly it bursts into flame. Everything the android touches starts to burn. Soon numerous fires pour billowing smoke into the cavern.

You can escape in the confusion, or try to put out the fire.

If you try to escape, turn to page 20.

If you try to put out the fire, turn to page 65.

46

You yell out a warning to Rebex and Qwoc. They turn to meet this new threat. The yellow lights solidify into the shape of a blond-haired, floppy-eared alien. He is humanoid in form, but his cat-shaped eyes have an orange glow.

Rebex squirts his protective fluid at the intruder. The blond alien falls unconscious. Rebex and Qwoc quickly bind him with anti-gravity cuffs, which raise the prisoner into the air.

"You think quickly, Earthling," Rebex says. "Thank you."

"Who is he?" you ask.

You hear a rumble, then Qwoc speaks to you using his communicator. His voice sounds like cement being poured. "He is a galactic constable. He has been chasing us for many light years. But never has he come so close to capturing us as he did today."

Rebex looks at the constable, who is slowly regaining consciousness. "Earthling, since you helped us catch him, it is only fitting that you should decide what we do with him." Rebex pulls out a wafer-thin, octagonal coin. "I will toss this coin. His fate is in your hands. Heads or tails?"

Rebex tosses the coin.

If you call heads, turn to page 113.

If you call tails, turn to page 93.

from page 29

You decide to greet the alien. "Wel-come to pla-net Earth," you say, figuring that aliens don't speak English too well.

"Thank you, Earthling," he says. "Fear not. I mean you no harm. I am Meglar from the star system Omicron."

This alien may speak English, but his lips don't move! "How did you do that?" you ask.

He laughs—a deep, rich sound that soothes you. "My race has no vocal chords. We communicate by directly transmitting our thoughts. Our scientists have been monitoring your radio broadcasts for many years. It's really quite simple."

As Meglar speaks, you notice that he is scratching his arms and legs. He glances down. Pointing in horror at the patch of poison ivy by his feet, he leaps backward.

"Earthling, I have been careless. To my people, this vegetation is a deadly poison. Its effects are immediate. I must have an antidote soon or I will die. Please help me."

Before you can answer, the alien passes out. You don't know what to do. Should you go into the spaceship? Maybe Meglar has companions.

Or should you go home for help?

If you go into the spaceship, turn to page 5.

If you go to get help, turn to page 40.

48

from page 57

Upon waking, you find yourself all alone in an empty, white room with no windows or doors. You wonder what happened to the alien. You call out to him, but no one answers.

The walls seem to absorb the sounds almost as soon as they leave your mouth. "There has to be a way out of here," you think. You proceed to examine the room.

The first thing you notice is that high in a corner there seems to be a kind of closed-circuit camera just like those in the bank. The camera is painted white and blends perfectly with its surroundings. The camera follows your every move.

You see a white button blending into the wall on your right. You press the button.

Turn to page 83.

"That was a foolish thing to do, Earthling. No one attacks me and lives. But I will make an exception in your case. You gambled when you tried to escape just now, so I propose a wager with you. If you can remain free on Earth for one hour while pursued by me and my men, I will free both you and your companions. If not . . . well, let us just say that capture will be unpleasant. What is your answer?"

You look at Rebex and Qwoc. Both are frozen in place. Zim's men are laughing, clearly enjoying your discomfort. You really have no choice but to agree.

Zim releases you and zaps you with a yellow light. The next thing you know, you are back on Earth, standing in front of an amusement park. A voice echoes in your ear.

"This is where your fate will be decided. You cannot leave the area. Force beams will seal you in. Remember, you must elude us for one hour."

Zim's men appear behind you, and you run into the park. You've lost them for the moment. But you have to find a hiding place. To your right is the Hall of Mirrors. To your left is the Fun House.

If you hide in the Hall of Mirrors, turn to page 97.

If you hide in the Fun House, turn to page 116.

from page 41

"I'll help you," you reply, "and I know where we can get the lead. My parents have some in our basement. It was once used for the piping in our house."

Meglar gets excited at this news. He presses his belt buckle, instantly transporting the two of you to your basement. It is dark down there. You look for the light.

"I have a light," Meglar replies. As he raises his palm, a glow illuminates the entire basement.

"How did you do that?" you ask.

"Never mind," says Meglar. "Where is the lead?"

You go to the work bench and there you see the old lead pipes neatly stacked on a lower shelf. You hand one to Meglar. He lowers his hand, leaving a glowing ball suspended in the air.

He examines the lead carefully, then cuts a length of it with a knifelike object.

"This is just what I need," says Meglar. "Come with me."

"But what about the light?"

Meglar clenches his fist and the room goes dark. In the next instant, the two of you are transported back to his ship.

Turn to page 22.

52

from page 19

You sprint for the wooden fence and try to get over it, but it is too high for you. You search frantically for something to use as a step. Just in time you spot a metal milk crate. It gives you the height you need.

As you try to swing over the fence, you slip and fall into a pile of junk on the other side. You've landed in the backyard of the abandoned house next door.

You struggle to free yourself, but trip over a rubber tire. You tumble forward into a plastic bag filled with garbage. Yuck!

You hear the growl of a dog from another yard, and a human voice calls out. "Hey you, what are you doing? Leave my dog alone. I'm calling the cops."

Something smashes against the fence behind you. The alien must be trying to scale it! You free yourself from the junk heap and run into the abandoned house.

You try to open the front door, but it's stuck. "Just my luck," you think and rush to the back door. It creaks as you open it. Now you just need a place to hide. To your right is a closet. Behind you is a staircase covered with dust.

If you hide in the closet, turn to page 76.

If you climb the stairs, turn to page 38.

You decide to help the robot. Suddenly its cries for help stop. You search the corner of the room where you last saw it. The room flashes green again, and this time fire hydrants are dropped into the chamber. They tumble to the ground, barely missing you.

You stumble over a metal toolbox and fall to the floor. You hear mumbling from beneath an air conditioner. You push it aside and see the robot.

"We have only two minutes before the room fills up completely. Press the button on my head device and hurrrrr...."

There are two buttons on the robot's toaster-oven head—one red and one black. The robot is silent. Which one do you press?

If you press the red button labeled "toast", turn to page 102.

If you press the black button labeled "top brown only", turn to page 24.

You wake up in a large underground chamber. Surrounding you are hundreds of aliens who all look the same. They are smiling at you.

One of them comes forward. Like the others, he has orange skin and is wearing a brown space suit. A bronze belt is tied snugly around his waist. But unlike the others, a green ball of fur hangs around his neck from a golden chain.

He speaks to you. "Welcome to my Earthbase."

"What am I doing here?" you ask. "And who are you?"

The ball around the alien's neck begins to glow. A disembodied voice echoes through the chamber. "I, Orv, am here to gather processed metal which my planet desperately needs to create a vaccine. It will enable me to fight a serious disease which threatens my people."

"What do you want with me?"

"Frankly, you are here by accident. My androids misinterpreted certain data and have brought me a life form instead of metal. They are an inefficient series, but I needed the use of their tentacles and arms for lifting. As you can see, I can't lift a thing on my own." The green ball glows brightly.

You are shocked to realize that the green ball of fur is an intelligent life form.

Turn to page 45.

from page 76

There's nowhere to run. You'll have to surrender to the alien. You wait for him to enter the closet, but suddenly the doorknob stops turning. Now you can see the light again beneath the door.

The footsteps move away from the door and grow faint. Then there is silence. You want to be sure that the alien is really gone, so you count to a hundred slowly. At the end of the count, you feel confident enough to risk peeking outside.

You ease the door open just a crack. There's no one there. You open it wider and see two sets of footprints in the dust. One set leads right into the closet. They're yours. The other set stops at the closet, continues a little way down the hall and then just stops. How can that be?

You emerge slowly from the closet. Your foot kicks something, sending it skittering across the floor. You walk over to it and see that it is a beautiful purple crystal.

As you bend down to pick it up, you are transported to the alien's spaceship orbiting Earth. You find yourself face to face with the orange-skinned alien.

"I've been waiting for you, Earthling. I believe that you have something that belongs to me."

Turn to page 73.

56

You race down the trail, quickly putting some distance between you and Meglar. Soon you are so tired you need a place to rest.

You spy a hollow log and crawl into it to catch your breath. Just as your breathing gets back to normal, you hear a voice echoing through the trees.

"Earthling, don't run. There are force fields set up to protect my ship. They are all around us and they are dangerous. Show yourself before it is too late."

This sounds like a trick. Until you can be sure, you decide not to show yourself. But what do you do next? Continue on the path? Or call Meglar's bluff and run through the brush toward his ship?

If you continue down the path, turn to page 103.

If you run toward his ship, turn to page 86.

You run away. Even though you feel sorry for the alien, the thought of his cold tentacle grasping you fills you with disgust. As you race through the next yard you hear a strange whirring sound behind you, followed by the irritated yelping of the dog.

Ahead lies the street. But your escape is brought to a sudden halt by yet another invisible barrier. You turn around and see the alien running after you. His tentacle is waving in the air above his head like a helicopter blade. He has two other humanlike arms wobbling at his sides. One of them is holding a tuning-fork-shaped device.

This tool emits a high-pitched whine that hurts your ears. As you try blocking the sound with your hands, the alien grabs you and holds you tight.

He stares at you with his huge eyes. It seems as though he can see right through you. "That beast would have had me back there, and you might have escaped, if not for my sonic sound distorter. A useful device." He brushes your head with his tentacle and you are suddenly tired.

In seconds you are sound asleep.

Turn to page 48.

from page 108

You take the passage to the right and walk until you come upon a clear plastic wall blocking the passageway. All you can see behind the plastic is an occasional flash of green. You decide to investigate. You trip an electric eye and the partition opens.

Behind the partition is a vast room filled with items of every description. There are clocks, radios, bicycles, cars, fences, and mailboxes—even a kitchen sink. A green flash appears again. When it disappears, the room is filled with rakes and shovels. "Wow," you think. "If this is the same beam that transported me here, maybe it can bring me back to Earth."

An object moving through this clutter attracts your attention. It's the robot who brought you the pills, and it is busy pushing the new acquisitions into the rising piles.

The green light flashes again, and heavy metal pipes fall into the chamber. You hear a loud crash. To your horror, the robot has been buried beneath it.

"Help me," cries the robot.

You want to help the kind robot. On the other hand, this could be your only chance to escape. But what if the beam is only a one-way transport system, from Earth to the ship? It could be dangerous.

The robot cries out again. What should you do?

If you try to transport yourself back to Earth by the beam, turn to page 35.

If you stay to help the robot, turn to page 53.

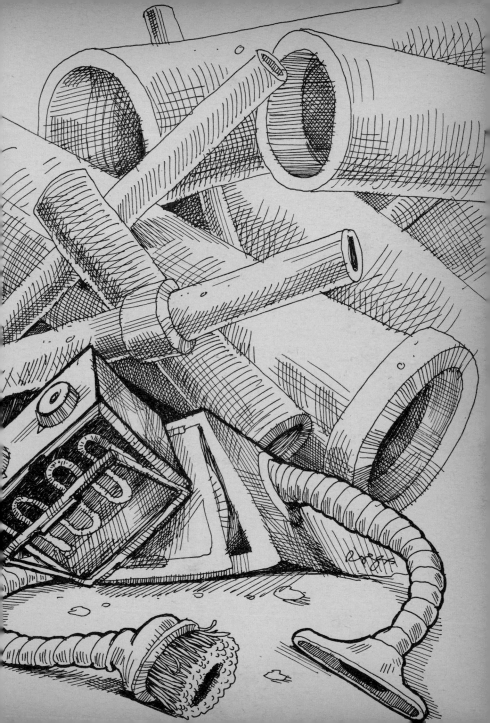

You remain hidden, trying to fight down your growing panic. The alien slowly advances into the garage, sweeping his eyes back and forth.

You shrink deeper into the shadows, hoping that he won't see you.

"I know you are here, Earthling," the alien says.

He could be bluffing. You don't move. The alien listens carefully to the silence. He stands very still and touches the tip of his tentacle to the top of his head. He starts spinning in a circle. He spins slowly at first, then blindingly fast. You blink, and he's gone!

With the door wide-open, sunlight streams into the garage. Your hiding place isn't dark any longer. You have to get out of here.

Outside is the driveway and the relative safety of the street. If you could only avoid the alien for just a little while longer, you might be able to make a break for home.

You step into the yard and look carefully around. It looks deserted.

Turn to page 68.

from page 27

You duck behind some metal boxes, then take a look back. The alien is gone! All you see is a glimpse of the brown mist floating toward you. It caught you once, but you resolve it won't catch you again.

Keeping ahead of the mist, you run to a jumble of stolen cars. Each time the brown mist strikes an object, the mist get thinner. You realize that its power weakens when it catches something.

Ahead of you is a pile of bicycles. You see your bike among them. If you could only reach your bike, you might be able to escape. Out of the corner of your eye, you spot the alien. He hides behind some clear, plastic globes. He isn't that far away.

You fling one of your glass discs at him. The disc hits the globes and makes them disappear. As the alien runs for cover, you throw your last disc. The alien sees it coming. Trying to get away, he trips and goes sprawling just as the disc strikes him. The alien vanishes!

Turn to page 109.

from page 5

You run back into the spaceship and stand before the computer. Maybe there is still a chance to save Meglar. The computer does not acknowledge your presence. Instead, it begins a countdown.

"Meglar inoperative. Activate self-destruct mechanism per program 5G. Twenty seconds to detonation. Nineteen, eighteen, seventeen, sixteen . . ."

You rush from the spaceship as fast as you can. But you can still hear the computer counting down. Jumping into a large ditch, you cover your head. "Have I gotten far enough away?" you wonder.

Behind you the computer drones on. "Eight, seven, six, five, four, three, two, one, zero."

At the count of zero, the whole clearing turns into a brilliant blaze of light. So does the ditch you hid in. "Guess I didn't get far enough," you think. And you're right. This is . . .

THE END

You press the black button and the pinpoint of light reappears. It quickly expands and the constable floats helplessly in midair.

Rebex lunges for you, and you barely escape his grasping claw. To defend yourself, you quickly search for some kind of weapon. You spot nothing except Qwoc's blazing eyes. That's it! Without wasting a second you grab Rebex's goggles and expose him to Qwoc's flaming eyes. Rebex is rendered helpless.

Qwoc lumbers toward you, his eyes blazing with rage. You shield your own eyes with Rebex's goggles. How can you get out of here? Suddenly, a flash fills the room. When you look, Qwoc is gone.

"Please get these restraints off me," calls out the constable from above. "I'm lucky I hit him with my electro-transfer generator. It's difficult to aim from up here, you know."

After you free the constable, he thanks you, then radios his ship for assistance.

"Don't worry about Qwoc," says the constable. "I've just imprisoned him. Again, thank you brave Earthling. Would you like to go home now?"

Before you can answer, a white mist floats around you.

Turn to page 112.

from page 45

You look for something to throw on the fire and find a bucket of clear liquid. You toss it on the fire, but it only makes the flames grow bigger.

Off to the left is a bucket of sand. You grab it, only to find the sand is surprisingly light. Just before you can toss it on the fire, Orv calls out from his burning android.

"Earthling, stop. Do not throw that on the fire. That is the vaccine I have been making. If you destroy it, all is lost. Use the canister beside you."

You use the canister to spray a pink mist over the flames. In minutes the fire is out. Smoke shrouds the chamber and some of the androids are still smoldering, but the danger is past.

"Are you all right?" you ask Orv.

"Yes, Earthling. But my android is useless. Would you please relocate me to another one?"

When the transfer is completed, you and Orv survey the damage. Numerous androids were destroyed, but none of the buckets containing the vaccine were harmed.

"Earthling, I am in your debt. Without your help, all would have been lost. You have great courage and compassion. This is not what we expected of your species. How can we repay you?"

Turn to page 80.

66

from page 69

The alien listens to your soft whistling with great interest. "Do all of you humans make these delightful sounds?" Before you can reply, the two of you are transported to the alien spaceship orbiting Earth.

"You must meet my companions," says Wulnar as he pulls you along. His tentacles feel creepy as they stick to your arm. He points to a nine-foot-tall lizard man covered with green scales. "This is Greela."

Greela's mouth opens, revealing a sharp set of green teeth. Beside Greela is a short, spiny creature resembling a porcupine, whom Wulnar introduces as Vag.

"These are my shipmates," says Wulnar. "A finer crew of thieves never existed. The metal we steal, we sell as scrap to cosmic junk dealers."

He brushes aside the questions of his crew and commands you to whistle. You do your best, under the circumstances. Greela smiles and closes his eyes, swaying in obvious delight. Vag seems to go into a pleasurable trance.

"Earthling," says Wulnar, "your sounds amuse us. It will be your good fortune to entertain us on our space travels. Now, let us hear that wonderful sound again."

You do your best as a cosmic canary. If you can amuse them long enough, maybe one day you can figure out a way to escape and return to Earth.

THE END

from page 113

You press the flashing blue button, but nothing happens!

Rebex quickly binds you with anti-gravity restraints. Within moments, you are floating around the bridge.

"Thank you, Earthling," says Rebex. "You have put the ship on automatic pilot. It's obvious that you are going to be a source of trouble and annoyance for us. You must be controlled."

He clamps a shiny collar around your neck. Rebex stands away from you and holds a box with a tiny antenna.

"From now on, you will be very cooperative."

He presses the button. Your mind is now under the control of the box. You eagerly await the commands of your new masters. You are a helpless drone.

THE END

As you run, a weird brown mist surrounds you. The mist feels so warm and secure that you feel like going to sleep.

In an instant, you are transported to an underground chamber in the alien's Earthbase. The orange-skinned alien stands before you.

"You have been quite troublesome, Earthling. I have wasted much time in tracking you down."

"Leave me alone," you say. "I didn't do anything to you."

"Quite right. But I need you in my experiment. I am a scientist from the planet Verda. I stole various Earth items before your eyes to see how you would react to these unexplained phenomena. I thought you would be interesting, but I'm afraid you Earthlings are thoroughly boring and predictable."

You have to think fast. Maybe if you are unpredictable he will let you go. You pull your hand out of your pocket and point it at the alien. You tell him that you will zap him if he doesn't let you go.

"You are bluffing, Earthling," says the alien.

If you try to convince the alien that you hold a dangerous weapon in your hand, turn to page 21.

If you fall to the ground and pretend you are crazy, turn to page 27.

Deciding to help the alien, you distract the dog by tossing the ball. The dog retrieves it. A few minutes later, the dog lies down, satisfied.

"Don't be afraid," you say to the alien in the tree. "The dog was only playing with you."

The alien speaks through a small mouth at the tip of a tentacled arm. "I have traveled all over the universe and I have never seen such a fierce creature. And such language! You should have heard what he was saying to me."

"You can speak to dogs?" you ask.

"My name is Wulnar Gad, and I can speak over nine thousand languages fluently. If you will be so kind as to move out of the way, I will get down."

The alien lowers himself from the branch, while keeping his three wary eyes on the sleeping dog. Then he grabs you with his tentacle. "Now come along with me, and no more tricks," he says.

As the ungrateful Wulnar Gad leads you away, you try attracting the dog's attention by whistling. It doesn't work. But your whistling *does* have a curious effect on the alien. Maybe you can escape if you can find out which kind of whistle upsets him.

If you whistle louder, turn to page 115.

If you whistle softer, turn to page 66.

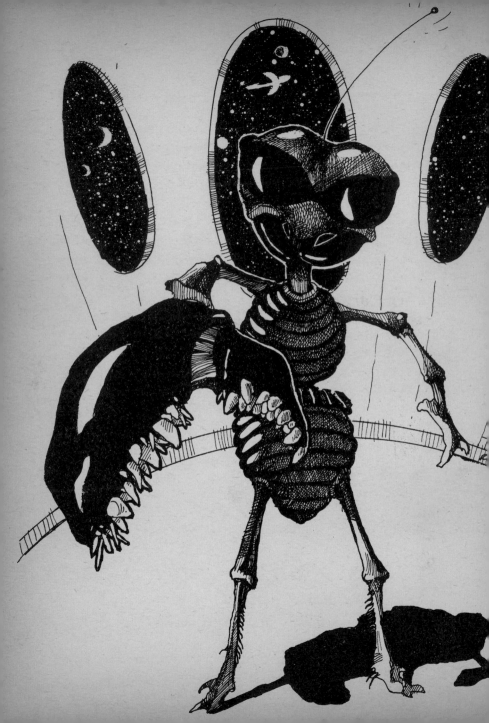

from page 26

You've been transported into some kind of strange room with several windows. Looking out the nearest window, you see the planet Earth several thousand miles away. You are aboard an alien space vessel!

Standing in front of you is a seven-foot-tall antlike creature. His eyes are covered by a set of goggles. His antenna waves back and forth as he studies you. He is standing upright on two sticklike legs. One of his arms has a fierce-looking claw that is pointing straight at you.

You hear a strange clicking sound. Perhaps the alien wants to communicate with you. You don't understand what he is saying, so you smile and wave a little. He cocks his head and pulls out a metal, pencil-shaped object from a pouch on his belt. He waves the object in circles, and soon the clicks become sounds you can understand.

"And what do we call you?" he asks.

Turn to page 81.

72

With the alien only a few feet away, you reach for the branch. Jumping up, you swing the branch like you would a baseball bat. The alien levitates himself to avoid your attack. Looks like the branch is not going to be so useful after all. You drop it.

The alien releases a red vapor that wraps itself around your body. You try to move your arms, but can't. You want to run, but your feet are locked in place. It feels as though you are wrapped in plastic.

The alien is standing before you. "Earthling, I tire of this chase. Escape is impossible. But I only want to talk. Then you may leave. I am called Meglar. What is your name?"

If you tell him your name, turn to page 41.

If you refuse to speak, turn to page 101.

"What are you talking about?" you ask the alien.

"The map. Where is the map?" As he questions you, the alien's huge eyes get red. "Answer me. Where is it?"

"I don't have any map," you say.

The alien snarls, contorting his face into a hideous mask. You shrink back. He pulls a weapon from his belt and fires a bolt of yellow energy at you. The bolt stuns you and knocks you to the ground.

The alien stands over you and starts searching through your clothing. The tentacle unties the laces on your sneakers. You don't know what he is searching for, but you don't say a word. He looks angry. He pulls your sneakers from your feet and examines the first one carefully, then tosses it over his shoulder. He glances at the sole of the second one, then hugs it to his chest and laughs.

"I've found it. I've found it," he cries. He dances a jig around the compartment of the ship. This may be your only chance to hide—while he is distracted. You narrow your escape routes down to two choices: a loose panel on an instrument bank, or a hatchway leading to a passage, on your left.

If you hide behind the bank of instruments, turn to page 84.

If you run for the hatchway, turn to page 94.

from page 9

"What are you talking about?" you ask.

"A comet is on a collision course with Earth," Meglar explains. "When it strikes your planet, the Earth will be destroyed. Nothing can stop the comet. But the people of Earth can be saved by taking them to another planet. To accomplish this mission, a vast fleet of spaceships is on its way.

"We of the Space Guardians do not want to cause a panic among the population of Earth," the alien continues. "So our search team selected you to be our spokesperson. But we must hurry. Time is running out."

"Why me?" you ask. "And why haven't I heard about this on the news?"

"Earthling," Meglar says, "your suspicions are irritating me. Don't you understand? Your planet is in grave danger. And we need an Earthling to speak for us. I need your answer now. Will you help me?"

If you find Meglar's story hard to believe and refuse to help him, turn to page 17.

If you accept his story and decide to help, turn to page 82.

Suddenly you hear a loud chuckle. Zim fires at you! The ray bounces off the mirror in front of you and zips back and forth around the maze.

In seconds, every mirror is destroyed. Then you hear a yelp of terror. Dozens of broken mirrors have collapsed on Zim, burying him. His legs are kicking in the air as though he is swimming.

As you run by him, he cries out. "Help me. I can't get out. Please help me." You still have time left, but you can't just leave him there. You carefully pull him out of the pile of glass by his legs.

When Zim sits up, he grabs your wrist, forcing you to drop the triangle. He pulls you toward him and stares into your eyes. For just a second you see the flicker of a smile, but it quickly vanishes.

"Earthling, you still have time left. Twenty seconds, to be precise. It looks like you've lost. But Syncron Zim repays his debts. Since you saved my life, you may go home. You and your companions are safe. Your kindness to me will not be forgotten. Thank you . . . friend."

THE END

76

from page 52

You open the closet and go inside, careful to close the door quietly behind you.

It's hot inside. Cobwebs brush against your face as you move deeper into the closet.

Your back is to the wall in the darkest corner of the closet. You keep your eyes fixed on the sliver of light coming from the bottom of the closed door. You bump your head into something metallic and hear a tinkling noise. You want to scream, but then you realize that it was only a wire hanger.

Footsteps echo in the old house. They get closer and closer. Something stops outside the closet, blocking out the light. You're not sure whether to surrender or fight. The doorknob starts to turn. You're trapped!

If you fight, turn to page 95.

If you surrender, turn to page 55.

from page 81

You put on the protective glasses. Everything looks purple.

"But who are you?" you ask.

"I am Rebex. And my companion is Qwoc. Despite his gentle appearance, Qwoc can be quite dangerous if you don't use these glasses."

"Why did you bring me here?" you ask.

"Qwoc?" says Rebex. "Would you care to explain?"

A loud rumbling fills the compartment as Qwoc speaks in a strange language.

"A malfunction?" says Rebex. "I thought you repaired the matter translocater."

Qwoc's red eyes glare.

"Calm down," Rebex says. "No offense was intended. But I do agree that the humanoid should be confined until we decide what to do with it."

Qwoc rumbles an acknowledgement, and Rebex turns toward you, squirting a jet of liquid from a spout just below his goggles. The liquid strikes you, and you lose consciousness.

Turn to page 100.

You ignore the ringing of the phone and race outside to help the alien. A few minutes after applying the lotion, Meglar stirs, then opens his eyes. He smiles at you.

"I owe you my life, Earthling. We now become brothers for all time." With his finger he traces a strange design on your forehead.

"Why did you come to Earth?" you ask.

"My mission is to chart human progress. It has been five hundred of your Earth years since we were last here. Much has changed. I was collecting samples when a malfunction in our retrieval circuits brought you here. Accidents are unfortunate, but I am glad that this accident happened."

"You're five hundred years old?"

"Actually, I am seven hundred and twenty of your Earth years old. We have slowed the aging process. Now, many of us live to ages of one thousand or more of your years."

"How long will you be here?"

The alien smiles and places his hand on your shoulder. "My mission is almost over. Would you like to come with me on a flight around the Earth?"

Turn to page 30.

You think for a moment. "I've never been very good in math, and tomorrow is my final exam. If I fail, I won't be allowed to go to the concert this weekend."

"Explain your mathematics to me. And what is a concert?"

When you explain to Orv, he chuckles. "That is simple, my young friend. Close your eyes and come close to me."

You feel a strange sensation as the android's hand traces a design on the top of your head. Your mind has never been so active. At long last, you understand algebra and trigonometry. You drift gently into a dreamless sleep.

When you wake up, you are home in bed. For the first time in your life, you are looking forward to taking a math test.

THE END

P.S. You get a perfect score.

You don't want to give your real name. But all you can think to say is, "I'm a news carrier."

"Really?" says the alien. He looks to his right and talks to a slab of stone. "Qwoc, you promised me riches if we came to rob Earth. But all we have so far is useless junk and a . . . news carrier!"

The slab of rock begins to move. It's alive! A pair of dark red eyes glow at you from the solid, gray mass.

"Earthling, don't gaze into his eyes," says the antlike creature. "Put on these protective glasses. Hurry."

If you put the glasses on, turn to page 77.

If you look into the eyes of Qwoc, turn to page 99.

from page 74

"I'll help you," you reply. "We've got to warn the mayor. He'll know what to do."

Meglar hits a button. Instantly, the two of you appear in the mayor's office. The mayor's not in, but you certainly scare his secretary. Before you can explain, two police officers burst into the room. They take you and Meglar prisoner.

"But I have come to warn you of a grave danger to your planet," Meglar protests. "A comet is going to collide with Earth."

"Sure it is, buddy," says one police officer. "Now just come along quietly with us." He turns to his partner. "Looks like we've got a live one here."

The peaceful Meglar does not resist. The two of you are brought to a holding room at the police station.

As you wait for your parents to come get you, you try to cheer up Meglar. "Don't worry," you say, "Mom and Dad will listen."

"We don't have time," Meglar says. "I've got to escape. Are you coming with me?"

It is a hard decision. What will you do?

If you agree to escape with Meglar, turn to page 90.

If you ask Meglar to wait a little bit longer, turn to page 8.

from page 48

The wall slides open and the alien comes striding into the room. "I see that you are awake," he says. His tone of voice is soft, yet you are still on your guard.

"Who are you?" you ask.

"I am Wulnar Gad and I am happy that you have recovered so quickly. Most beings are unconscious for days after my tentacle touches them. You have only been unconscious for two hours. Are all Earthlings as strong as you?"

You don't answer the alien. The lower part of his face crinkles into a kind of smile. The effect makes him uglier than before. You shiver at the sight of him.

"Be silent if you wish, Earthling. There is plenty of time for us to talk. Come with me."

If you go with him, turn to page 118.

If you resist, turn to page 14.

from page 73

You crawl into the instrument bank and hide, trying to figure out what to do next. The alien suddenly lets out a bellow of rage. The cabin of the ship fills with a bright white light and you are lifted into the air.

The alien stands before you. "I have searched for this map for years. Now that I have it, I will never give it up. Didn't you think I would find it?"

"What are you talking about? And give me back my sneakers."

"Never. Ah, but you are clever, Draxus. Concealing the map in the pattern on the sole of this foot-covering. And what a brilliant disguise! You look just like an Earthling, but you can't fool me."

You tell him that you don't know what he's talking about, but the alien refuses to listen. He mumbles about robberies and about a hidden treasure. He points his tentacle at you and you spin in the air like a top. The alien laughs long and loud. You realize he is crazy, and you cry out for help.

The alien stops you from spinning. "Draxus, we were once friends. Why did you betray me to the space police? Ten solar years I spent on that penal planet, while you roamed free. I vowed to get revenge. And now it's mine. Goodbye, Draxus."

You realize that this terrible case of mistaken identity will be . . .

THE END

86

You run in the direction of Meglar's ship. Not realizing that your sneakers have come untied, you trip over your laces. You stumble into the remains of a rickety, old fence, snapping the top rung into two pieces. One piece of wood vanishes in a puff of smoke not five feet from where you have fallen. The other piece of wood lands in the field on the other side of the fence.

"Meglar was telling the truth," you say to yourself. The force field is there, but it stops only a few feet from where you are standing. Perhaps you should trust him. But why is he hiding in the woods if he is friendly? You must get help.

Keeping your eyes on the piece of wood, you run ahead carefully. As long as you run a straight line you will avoid the force field.

Turn to page 117.

from page 93

You and the constable untangle yourselves from one another inside the small capsule.

You are the first one to speak. "I'm sorry. I didn't know who you were."

The constable speaks to you, and his voice is surprisingly deep and mellow. "Do not worry. All is not as it seems."

"But we're trapped in space. We don't even know where we are."

"It is not necessary to know where you are," says the constable. "You must only make sure that others do."

"I don't understand."

"Rebex and Qwoc are very good at being thieves. They have been partners for many years. But they are also rather stupid. They neglected to search me." The constable pulls a ring from one of his fingers. "This is a directional homing device. At this moment it is sending signals to my own ship. We will be rescued shortly."

"What about Rebex and Qwoc?" you ask.

"Before I was neutralized by Rebex, I dropped a homing device on the deck," says the constable. "They won't get far."

Soon you'll be on your way home. What a story you'll have to tell.

THE END

88

from page 37

You crouch down and get ready to run by the alien. Your knee touches a brick. If you throw the brick at the pile of flower pots in the corner, the noise might distract the alien long enough for you to escape.

Unfortunately, the brick slightly scrapes the floor as you pick it up. The alien points his weapon right at you. You see a great golden ball come flashing towards you.

The ball strikes the automobile, causing it to glow brightly. Then the car disappears. There is now nothing between you and the alien. You raise the brick to defend yourself, but a charge of pure energy strikes you and knocks you unconscious.

Turn to page 54.

from page 38

You remain silent as the alien walks up to your hiding place. His eyes are glowing in the darkness.

"Why did you run, Earthling? I meant you no harm."

"You frightened me," you reply.

"I am sorry. I forget that my appearance can be upsetting to humans. But all I wanted was some food. My ship was damaged during a magnetic space storm and none of my systems has worked properly ever since.

"While I was inspecting my transporter circuits, the system malfunctioned, sending me to Earth. You ran away before I could explain. Please accept my apologies. Your vehicle will be returned to you. My people are not thieves."

He pulls a blue stone from a pouch on his belt. "Here is payment for what I took. It is a Colibrius stone. Its heat can cook a meal, but not burn your skin. It can warm your living unit on the coldest nights and cool it on the warmest days. To command it, simply hold it in your hands and project your thoughts. It will obey. Goodbye."

The alien vanishes. In his place is a pale-blue, marble-shaped stone. You hold the stone in your hand and stare into its blue depths. It is hot in the old house and you wish for a breeze. The stone glows brightly and a refreshing coolness washes over you.

Wait till your friends and family see this— and wait till they hear this story!

THE END

from page 82

"I'll escape with you," you say. "But how are we going to get out of here?"

"Stand with me," says Meglar. He presses his belt buckle, transporting the two of you to the bridge of his spaceship. He sits in a chair in front of the instrument console and puts his head in his hands.

"I have bungled this mission," says Meglar. "We have so little time before the comet strikes. I have failed. Your planet will be destroyed."

"Wait a minute," you say. "You told me that nothing can stop the comet. But what if you deflect the comet off course by firing your spaceship's weapons at it?"

Meglar looks at you with respect. "A good idea. Let's check its probability of success with the computer." Moments later, Meglar has his answer.

"It just might work," he says. "But the odds against it are a million to one. Still it must be tried. It is Earth's last chance."

Watching the viewing screen, you see bursts of energy strike the comet. Meglar whoops and claps his hands. "We've done it! The comet's trajectory has been altered. It will miss Earth by two thousand miles. You are a hero, Earthling."

As Meglar shakes your hand, you know you have found a friend for life.

THE END

from page 14

You stand up and face the alien, determined to fight him. But he points a coin-shaped object at you.

Silver strands fly from the coin, binding your hands and feet securely. Wulnar reaches out and grabs you by the shirt, pulling you close to him so that you are staring into his three eyes.

"I may be just a common thief, Earthling, but I can recognize courage when I see it. In some parts of the galaxy, they pay very well for beings with courage. On Varex, they would train you to be a fierce warrior. You would fight to the death for the amusement of the great leaders. On Tremlin, you could be used to work the zirconium mines. On Delph, I'm sure the scientists could use you for their experiments . . ."

You struggle against your bonds as the alien drones on about the many planets where you could be useful. Then he tosses you to the ground like a rag doll.

"Stop struggling, Earthling. You will never escape." He presses a button on a silver box, and the bonds turn into a shield that covers you from head to toe. You can't keep your eyes open.

"You will sleep now, Earthling. And when you awaken, you will be at your new home." The last thing you hear is Wulnar's grunts of laughter.

THE END

"Tails," you say.

"Tails it is," says Rebex as he looks at the coin. He shakes his head sadly. "I was afraid of that."

"What?" you ask.

"You just chose to have the good constable placed in a capsule and jettisoned into space. Qwoc, prepare him."

Qwoc roughly grabs the constable, removes the anti-gravity restraining devices, and stuffs him inside a space capsule.

"That's terrible," you say.

"Oh, it's not so bad. He'll have company—you. We can leave no witnesses." Rebex grabs you and stuffs you into the capsule, too.

The panel is closed, and you are propelled into the depths of space.

Turn to page 87.

You run for the hatchway and are nearly there when the alien cries, "Stop!" Before you can reach the passageway on the other side, the hatchway slams closed. You crash into the hatch and lose consciousness.

When you open your eyes, the alien is standing over you. "You can't escape," he says. "It is useless to try."

"Who are you?" you ask. "And what do you want with me? I have nothing that you would want."

The alien laughs. "Ah, but you do. My name is Wulnar Gad. Last year a space criminal stole a shipment of valuable metal from a space freighter. He hid the shipment on Earth and drew a map of its location before being captured by the space police. The police interrogated him, but he never told them where he hid the metal."

"What has that got to do with me?" you ask.

"He hid on Earth before his capture. Just before he was taken prisoner, he secretly camouflaged the map as a pattern on the sole of an Earthling's footwear. It was in your possession."

"I don't believe you. How do I know you are telling the truth?"

"Because I am that criminal." The alien holds up a weapon. "Don't worry," he says. "You won't feel a thing."

THE END

from page 76

You're ready to fight. You grab the wire hanger. As the door opens, a flashlight shines in your face.

"What's going on here?" It's a policeman.

You're so happy to see him that you hug him, then blurt out your story. "There was this alien chasing me. He looked real weird. He had this tentacle, and this green ray made my bike disappear."

"Just a minute. I don't know anything about any green rays. All I know is we got a call from the owner of the house next door. He said some kids were teasing his dog. Now, where's your friend?"

"Wait a minute, officer. He's not my friend. I told you he was chasing me and . . ."

The police officer sighs. "Okay, suit yourself. I was just going to let you off with a warning. But since you won't tell me the truth, I'll have to take you in to the station house. Are you sure you don't want to tell me where your friend is? We'll find him sooner or later."

As he leads you away, you wonder how you are ever going to get anyone to believe you.

THE END

from page 49

You race into the Hall of Mirrors with the aliens in hot pursuit.

Scampering quickly through the maze, you try to slip out the back. When you go through the door, you see a bright light materializing. It's Zim!

Zim spots you and fires a golden beam at you. A mirror crashes over your head. You race through the maze, hoping to keep away from the other aliens inside. On the floor you see a platinum triangle that must have been dropped by one of the aliens. You pick it up. If you can figure out how to operate it, maybe you can escape.

Standing in front of you is one of Zim's humanoids. His back is to you. Your fingers feel a trigger mechanism on the triangle. You aim it at the alien, hoping that you are holding it the right way.

You fire and the alien is encased in blue webbing. You did it! Now you have a chance. The aliens seem disoriented by the Hall of Mirrors. You easily surprise the other three. Now only Zim remains. You have less than two minutes to go. Can you make it the full hour?

Turn to page 75.

from page 19

You try to go around the dog, but he growls and shows his teeth each time you come near. You see a tattered ball nearly hidden by the grass in the backyard. The dog is watching you carefully. You know the alien can't be far behind.

You pick up the ball and the dog crouches, his eyes riveted on the ball in your hand. He's no longer growling, and his short tail is playfully flicking back and forth. You throw the ball over the dog's head and he leaps for it, catching it in his mouth.

Since the dog is preoccupied with the ball, you risk racing for the open gate. But the dog growls and leaps in front of you with the ball in his teeth. He drops the ball at your feet.

You glance over your shoulder and see the alien materializing in the backyard, one limb at a time. You slowly reach for the ball and throw it over your shoulder, right at the alien. The dog zips past you, leaping into the air while you run for the open gate.

Turn to page 10.

You look directly into Qwoc's eyes. Then something funny happens. You can't remember your name. You stare at your hands, unsure of what they are or what they do. When you look down at your feet, you laugh hysterically. They seem so funny-looking. You take a deep breath and forget to exhale, causing you to faint.

When you wake up, Rebex is by your side. His goggles look weird. He puts a set of goggles on you just as Qwoc rumbles into your line of sight.

Rebex is concerned. "Earthling, I warned you not to look into the eyes of Qwoc. They will steal your memories. That is why you must always use these shielded goggles when he is present. How do you feel now?"

"I'm okay," you reply. "What are you going to do with me?"

Rebex laughs. "Nothing. We're going to send you home. Qwoc and I are on a cosmic scavenger hunt. The last thing we had to obtain was two tons of Earth items. When our matter translocater—the green ray— indicated a life form, we decided to have some fun with you by saying we were bandits."

"Do you mean I can go?" you ask.

"Absolutely. We'll return you to your planet and we'll go on our way."

"What about those things you stole?"

Turn to page 25.

100

A loud clattering noise awakens you, and you see a startling sight. Leaning over you is a weird-looking robot. He has a toaster oven for a head and a washing machine for a body. Two vacuum-cleaner hoses wobble at its side like arms.

"Would you care for some sustenance?" the robot asks.

"What do you have?" you ask.

The door of the toaster oven drops open and a plate slides out. On it are two pills. One is red and yellow. The other is shiny gray. The pills don't look appetizing, but you are awfully hungry.

Turn to page 108.

from page 72

You refuse to tell the alien anything. Now Meglar is growing angry. "On my planet, Earthling, it is an insult not to give your name when it is asked for."

When you still remain silent, Meglar turns from you and begins spinning like a top. The red vapor that binds you vanishes. Then an emerald crystal comes flying from the spinning alien. When you catch it, the crystal begins to glow brightly.

The glow becomes a glare, and you feel light-headed. Slowly turning your eyes away from the jewel, you look down. No wonder you're dizzy. You've been lifted twenty feet off the ground! Soon you're thirty feet in the air. There is nothing but the emerald crystal keeping you from falling. You clutch it tightly.

Meglar chuckles. The crystal's brightness dims and you are gently lowered to the ground.

"Do not be so strong-willed, Earthling. There are others who possess powers that you can only dream about. If you choose not to reveal your name, so be it. Now come with me."

Somehow you know that if Meglar really wanted to know your name, he could get it from you. You have no choice but to follow him to his ship.

Turn to page 43.

from page 53

You press the red button. "Thank you," the robot replies. "You have activated my strength mechanism. I will now be able to free myself. Move away, please, or you may be hurt."

You back away from the robot as he throws the air conditioner high into the air. The pipes follow. In seconds, the robot is standing upright in a clear space.

The robot rolls toward you. "A robot's primary function is to serve. Since I am a Class 5 in the Upper Semilon Series, I am programmed to evaluate my master.

"I am presently utilized by thieves. This is counter to my programmed values. I have been unable to escape until now. When you risked your own safety to assist me, I sensed that you are a worthy master. My previous programming is cancelled. I am yours to command."

"Where am I?" you ask.

"You are in a storage bay of a proton-powered space vehicle of the Beta 28 Class. We are orbiting Earth."

"I want to go home," you say. "How can I get out of here?"

"Follow me."

The robot wheels away. Can you trust him?

Turn to page 36.

from page 56

You continue down the path. The trail narrows until your shirt is snagging on thorny bushes. But you are determined not to let anything stop you.

Ahead of you, the path widens. Now it is easier to run again. Suddenly, you find yourself on a well-traveled path. You hear the roar of automobiles and realize that you are near a main road. As you round a bend in the path, you see cars speeding by.

You've made it! Now you can get help. You run as fast as you can. Suddenly, you notice a shimmer in the air in front of you. It's some kind of energy field! You try to put on the brakes, but you can't stop. You strike the force field and vanish in a puff of smoke.

THE END

104

You take the left corridor, toward the hum of machinery. You pass many compartments overflowing with clothes hangers, bottles, jars, curtains, bath mats, and bathtubs.

The sound grows louder and louder. You cautiously advance. Soon the noise is almost deafening. You peek around the open doorway and see Qwoc lying on a metal slab. Huge pistons are pounding him on his back. Sighs of contentment are coming from Qwoc. You realize that he is getting a mechanical massage.

You giggle. Qwoc sits up and turns in your direction. Red beams glow from his eyes.

Turn to page 99.

106

from page 43

Branches clutch at your clothes as you crash through the brush. You pull free with a tremendous effort and run ahead, unsure of where to go next.

Faster and faster you run, until you trip over a tree root. You land hard in a gully. When you try to stand, your left leg won't support you.

"Do not move, Earthling." It's Meglar.

"Now I've had it," you think.

The alien is floating above you. Again he releases the red vapor. But this time, the red mist transforms into a stretcher and gently returns you to the spaceship.

Once inside, Meglar lays you on a table that moves through a tunnel-shaped device. White light bombards your leg. When you emerge, you find you can walk perfectly. You thank Meglar. Now you tell him your name. "What do you want with me?" you ask.

"I am lonely and I wanted a companion," Meglar says. "So I stole things with my transporter, hoping to catch someone with whom I could speak. Instead, all I got were useless items that I couldn't identify, and a furry creature who communicated in a primitive barking language. It has been a long time since I last spoke to someone. Can't you spend a few moments with me?"

Turn to page 111.

Meglar records the formula onto a cassette. He says you can play the cassette on a simple recorder. It will outline the steps necessary to convert water into fuel.

"Now, I must leave you. My mission is behind schedule. If my circuits didn't burn out, I never would have come to Earth. I never meant to frighten you. Goodbye!"

Meglar presses his belt buckle and transports you to the start of your paper route. In the distance, you hear a loud roar and see a streak of light shooting straight into the air.

You rush home, anxious to try out the formula. When you play the cassette on your parents' stereo, you are surprised that the instructions are so easy.

You test a batch of fuel in the power lawn mower. It works! As you rush off to tell your family, you wonder how it will feel to go down in history as the person who solved the energy shortage.

THE END

108

You take the pills and hold them in your hands. "What are they?" you ask.

"I believe that the red and yellow one is identified as pizza. And the gray one is a cola beverage."

"You're kidding," you say.

"I do not understand this 'kidding' of which you speak."

"You know—tell a joke. Play a trick."

The robot seems to be thinking. "These words are not in my memory banks," it says. "Should you require more sustenance, I will return." It moves away on rollers as you call after it.

"Wait. What am I supposed to do?"

"You are free to roam the ship, with one restriction. Stay away from the corridors with red markings on the floor." The robot speeds away.

You pop the pills in your mouth. Amazing! They actually taste like pizza and soda. You rush down the passageway hoping to find the robot. But he is nowhere to be seen.

You decide to explore the ship. In front of you the corridor branches right and left. To the left, you hear the hum of machinery. To the right, there is silence. You see no red markings anywhere.

Which way do you go?

If you take the right corridor, turn to page 58.

If you take the left corridor, turn to page 104.

You stand up, only to find yourself trapped in an invisible box. The alien appears in front of you. "But I thought I made you disappear," you say.

"You did," says the alien. "But I can reappear at will by activating the materializer on my belt. You've done well, Earthling. Better than most other beings. You will make an interesting subject."

As he speaks, two other aliens materialize in the chamber. One looks like a bird with human arms. The other looks like a piece of gnarled wood.

"What do you want with us?" you shout.

"In my numerous experiments, there are three species which have proved the strongest and most adaptable—the bird people of Sirriu, the Treelites of Simlac 10, and the human beings of Earth. In a few moments I will place the three of you in a maze with only one exit.

"Inside the maze will be items stolen from various planets in the galaxy. Some items are quite harmless. Others might help you to escape. A few are quite deadly. Only one of you can win. The others will perish."

"But I'm only a news carrier," you protest. "Why are you doing this to me?"

"For science. Now let the games begin."

THE END

You reach for the flat stone as the alien closes in on you. "Stay away," you shout. But he ignores you. You throw the stone at him, hoping to frighten him away.

The stone just misses and the alien ducks. Here's your chance to escape! You run for it.

The alien pulls a weapon from his belt and fires.

All his shots miss you. But they are close enough to make the air crackle as the rays zip by you. Ahead of you is the safety of the woods. If you could only make it there, you could hide. The alien would never find you.

You glance over your shoulder and see the alien trip over a tree branch, and fall to the ground. Diving forward, you land in the brush. You hear the alien crashing through the brush searching for you. But you stay perfectly still until the sounds fade in the distance.

You wait until you're sure it's safe, then you crawl from your hiding place. You run all the way home, keeping to the shadows and crouching behind parked cars. Safely in your house, you wonder why the alien was after you. You hope you never find out.

THE END

You are curious about Meglar's home planet, and you ask him about it.

"My planet is called Zenon 5, because it is the fifth planet from the red sun Zenon."

The two of you are sitting under a tree when it starts to rain. When the first drop strikes Meglar, he leaps to his feet and tries to collect the rain in the pouches of his belt. As it rains harder, Meglar grows more frantic. He leaps from spot to spot trying to capture all the raindrops. In a few minutes, he is exhausted. He lies on the ground and the rain soaks him thoroughly. When the shower ends, Meglar stands and grins sheepishly.

"Your planet is mostly water," he says. "Mine is nearly all land. Since water is so scarce on our world, it has become a source of great wealth and power. I had heard of the great wealth of your planet, but I never believed it until now. To have water fall from the sky . . . you are the luckiest of planets."

You feel sorry for Meglar. Then you get an idea. You sneak Meglar home and fill several bottles of water from the sink. You give Meglar the water as a present. He returns to Zenon 5, a wealthy traveler.

THE END

from page 63

You are sitting under a tree with a gentle breeze blowing on your face. Your bicycle is lying beside you, and your news sack has spilled its papers all over the grass.

What a crazy dream that was, you think, until you see the constable standing in front of you.

"Earthling, you gave me back my life after those thieves nearly took it. Now I give you something."

It is a plastic cube.

"Thank you," you say. "But what is it?"

The constable smiles. "It is a thought projector. To operate it, simply hold the cube in your hand and think of what you wish to see. A three-dimensional projection of your thoughts will result. You'll find it marvelous when you read. Goodbye, my friend."

THE END

"Heads," you say as Rebex catches the coin.

"It's tails," replies Rebex. "The constable loses."

Qwoc's laughter rumbles through the bridge like an earthquake. Rebex sits behind the instrument panel and presses four buttons. The air around the constable seems to get thick.

Two white lines trace a square around the constable. Rebex pushes a lever and the box shrinks until both the constable and the box are a mere pinpoint of light. Then, the light blinks out and they are gone.

"He's gone," you think. "I've got to save him."

"Hey, wait a minute," you call out, rushing toward the instrument panel. "What did you do with him?"

You push Rebex away from the instrument panel and stare at all the buttons and lights in front of you. Maybe if you press the right buttons you can get him back. Within your reach are a rectangular black button and a flashing blue button.

But you're running out of time. Rebex is lunging at you.

Which button do you choose?

If you press the rectangular black button labeled "BACYANC", turn to page 63.

If you press the flashing blue button labeled "AW2PYLET", turn to page 67.

from page 21

A second alien appears in the chamber. This one is short, chunky, and has brown quills like a porcupine. He releases you from the brown mist.

"I am a friend, Earthling. Do not worry; your finger is harmless now. When I realized what you had planned, I decided to give you the power to make it work."

"Do you mean, my finger didn't really fire?" you ask.

"No. It was just an illusion."

"Why did you help me?"

"My colleague here has long bragged that he is a superior scientist. He has traveled the universe staging these stupid tests of his. He always claims that he is stealing just to test the reactions of his subjects. But lately he has kept what he has taken for his own profit. I could not let him continue."

"What will happen to him now?" you ask.

"He will be given the very best treatment, and one day he will be able to resume his place in the scientific community. Goodbye, Earthling. Thank you for helping me teach my colleague a valuable lesson."

THE END

You whistle long and loud.

"Please stop that irritating noise," says Wulnar. "It bothers me."

"Let me go," you say. "I don't want to go with you."

"Well, why didn't you say so? Never let it be said that Wulnar Gad ever held anyone against his will."

"Who are you?" you ask.

"I am a collector, and I have visited your fair planet to accumulate items for a show that I am putting on."

"But you're stealing them."

"Details, details. I do not understand what you mean. What is this thing called stealing?"

When you explain to him what stealing means, the alien looks insulted.

"I have chosen you, Earthling, to be the first of any species to view my masterpiece. It is a collection of Earth items tastefully arranged in an artistic design. But since you refuse this golden opportunity, I will have to leave." The alien vanishes.

A minute later you find yourself surrounded by fences, bicycles, mailboxes, automobiles, lawn furniture, and swing sets. You look up when a truck driver blows his horn at you. His truck can't pass.

"Hey," he yells, "move this junk out of here. What are you trying to do anyway? Start a recycling center?"

You wonder what Wulnar has planned for his next show.

THE END

116

from page 49

You run into the Fun House. Two aliens are close behind you. Having been to this amusement park before, you know that the first room in the Fun House has thick foam-rubber flooring. It is almost impossible to stay on your feet, so you fall to your knees and crawl to the next room.

Now the aliens storm into the room. "Help!" they cry in surprise. As they struggle to regain their balance, one of them accidentally fires his paralyzer. He freezes his companion. There is now only one chasing you.

The next room has a tilted floor and can only be crossed by holding the handrails. You've nearly made it to the other side when the alien stumbles into view. "Yow!" He slides down the tilted floor and bangs against the lower wall. He is unconscious. You take his weapon and secure his belt tightly around your waist.

Suddenly a third alien appears in the doorway. You barely avoid the jet of hot air that shoots from his weapon. The blast strikes the wall behind you and burns a hole through it.

You fire your weapon, and the recoil knocks you backward. The shot misses the alien, but it does knock loose a chunk of ceiling. The chunk pins down the frustrated alien. You head for the room of darkness and wait.

Turn to page 32.

from page 86

When you reach town, you tell Police Captain Magee what happened. He has received an unusually high number of burglary reports. Captain Magee doesn't know whether to believe your wild story. But since he has no other leads on the stolen property . . .

When you get to the woods with the police, the spaceship is gone. Captain Magee isn't surprised. "But it was here!" you insist. Then you look down.

Beneath your feet is a large patch of burned ground. Captain Magee sees this, too. After searching the area, you find much of the stolen property hidden in the bushes.

A loud roaring sound makes everyone look up. Meglar's spaceship hovers overhead. In a flash, the ship shoots straight up and vanishes. Captain Magee is speechless. You wonder if he'll believe your story now.

THE END

118

You follow the alien into a huge underground cavern. The hum of machinery fills the room, and you can feel a breeze blowing against your face.

In front of you are high piles of objects. As you get closer you see radios, television sets, clothes, bicycles, cars, and even a city bus. It's as though you are in a huge warehouse.

"What is all this?" you ask.

"Impressive, isn't it?" replies Wulnar with obvious pride. "Your planet is incredibly rich, and I will become a wealthy Globulan after this job."

As Wulnar tells you about himself, you learn he is a common thief from the planet Globula. He has been systematically looting the Earth for years. He values anything that he can sell on other planets.

A green beam deposits a garbage truck right in front of you. Wulnar is pleased with his catch and examines the contents of the truck. Whenever he touches a piece of garbage, he clucks with satisfaction. He turns to you.

"My transporter circuits are programmed to bring me all valued objects caught in its beam. But a warning alarm sounded when it registered a life-form reading. I have always been curious about Earthlings, but now that you are here, what am I going to do with you? No one has ever witnessed my thefts before."

Turn to page 42.